No TV

Written by Jill Eggleton
Illustrated by Rob Kiely

Rigby

The people in the book

Jack and his mom

Finn and his dad

Lee and Sam's family

Carlo's family

The place
in the book

Sun Sun House

It's Friday night.
The kids in Sun Sun House
are watching TV.

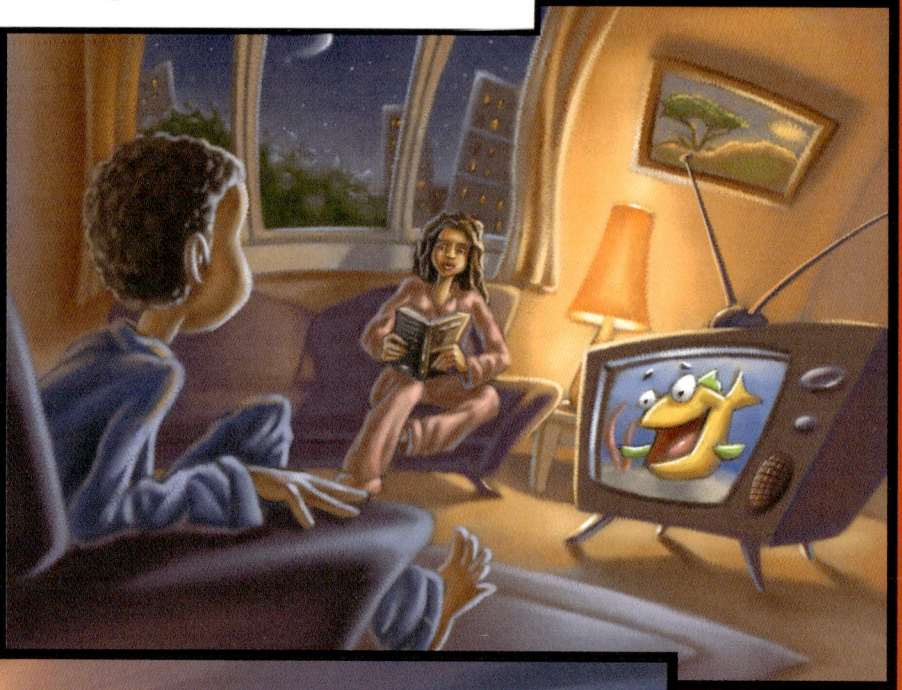

Then...

in Jack's house the TV went...

BANG!

Jack's mom looked at the TV.

"I can't fix it," she said.

"No TV! But I like TV," said Jack.

"I will tell you a story," said his mom.

"A story is not as good as TV," said Jack.

Jack's mom went away.
When she came back,
she had a big bag.

She took out some **pink** hair
and a **green** coat.
She put on the hair
and the coat.

Jack's mom will tell...

a funny story?

a sad story?

Jack's mom sat down
and she told a story.
Jack laughed and laughed and laughed!

There was a

KNOCK,

KNOCK,

KNOCK

on the door.

Jack went to the door.
He saw...

Lee

Sam

Carlo

Finn

The kids came over to...

watch TV?

hear a story?

The kids came into Jack's house. They all sat down.

Jack's mom got glasses and a nose. She put on the glasses and the nose.

Then she told a story.
The kids laughed and laughed
and laughed!

It's Saturday night.
The kids in Sun Sun House
are **not** watching TV.

The kids in Sun Sun House are making up stories!

The End

Mapping chart

The cat went into the box.

The giant had a big ice-cream cone.

The monkey went up the tree.

The crocodile went, "Snap, snap, snap!"

Word Bank

bag

coat

door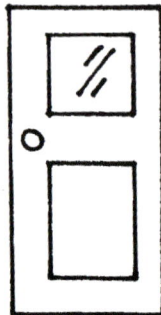